Song for Papa Crow

Written and Illustrated by
Marit Menzin

Schiffer Publishing Ltd®

4880 Lower Valley Road • Atglen, PA 19310

Copyright © 2012 by Marit Menzin
Library of Congress Control Number: 2012938439

Designed by Danielle D. Farmer
Type set in Artistik/TimesScrDLig

ISBN: 978-0-7643-4131-1
Printed in China

Schiffer Books are available at special discounts for
bulk purchases for sales promotions or premiums.
Special editions, including personalized covers,
corporate imprints, and excerpts can be created
in large quantities for special needs. For more
information contact the publisher:

Published by Schiffer Publishing, Ltd.
4880 Lower Valley Road
Atglen, PA 19310
Phone: (610) 593-1777; Fax: (610) 593-2002
E-mail: Info@schifferbooks.com

For the largest selection of fine reference books
on this and related subjects, please visit our
website at www.schifferbooks.com
We are always looking for people to write books
on new and related subjects. If you have an idea
for a book, please contact us at proposals@
schifferbooks.com

This book may be purchased from the publisher.
Please try your bookstore first.
You may write for a free catalog.

In Europe, Schiffer books are distributed by
Bushwood Books
6 Marksbury Ave.
Kew Gardens
Surrey TW9 4JF England
Phone: 44 (0) 20 8392 8585;
Fax: 44 (0) 20 8392 9876
E-mail: info@bushwoodbooks.co.uk
Website: www.bushwoodbooks.co.uk

DEDICATION

This book is dedicated
to my children, Orly, Ion, and Daniel,
and to my husband, Larry,
with all my love.

Little Crow loved to sing.
He sang all the time, everywhere he went.

"Caw! Caw! Caw!"
he croaked.
The singing birds did not love to hear Little Crow sing.
Not any time. Not anywhere.

Whenever Little Crow joined them in the big old maple tree,
he saw them leave, one by one.

"*Per-CHIC-o-ree!*"
sang the Goldfinches. "Let's try another tree."

"Fee-beee,"
said Phoebe Flycatcher. "Be quiet. You'll scare away my lunch."

"*What-CHEER!*"
cheeped Red Cardinal. "Got to go!"

And so Little Crow was left to sing alone.

"Here you are," said Papa Crow. "I followed your lovely song."

"Papa," said Little Crow, "the other birds don't like my singing."

"Don't listen to them. Sing a song for Papa. When I hear your sweet caw, I can find you anywhere."

The next day, Papa Crow had a surprise.

"Cheer up, Little Crow," Papa said.

"Look at the signs. The Amazing Mockingbird is in town for one show only."

When night came, Papa and Little Crow went to see the show.
Blue Jay was the security. "*Too-loo,*" he called, keeping
away hawks and eagles.

"Hoot? Who?"
asked the owls.

"It's the Amazing Mockingbird,"
announced Bluebird.

The hummingbirds hummed, dancing
backwards through the air.

The woodpeckers drummed their beaks on the trunk of the tree.

Mockingbird hummed and drummed.
"*Per-CHIC-o-ree!*"
sang Mockingbird.

"That's our favorite song,"
said the finches.
"*Fee-beee!*" he sang next.

"*Oooh!*" said Phoebe Flycatcher.
"He is so good!"

"*What-CHEER!*"
sang Mockingbird.

"I think I might faint,"
said Cardinal.

Then, Mockingbird sang all night until the sun came up,
"*Whip-poor-will,
whip-poor-will.*"

After the show, Little Crow asked Papa
to take him to Mockingbird's tent for an autograph.
"Did you enjoy the show?" asked Mockingbird.

"Oh yes! I wish I could mimic the other birds just like you."

"You know, someone just sent me some sort of whistling seeds.
They're supposed to help with singing,
but I haven't tried them yet," said Mockingbird.
"Oops, I shouldn't have said that."

"Please, Mockingbird," asked Little Crow,
"do you have an extra seed for me?"

"You don't need a seed," said Papa.
"When I hear your sweet caw, I know just where you are."

"But I need that seed!" said Little Crow.
"I want to sing like the other birds."

"You are a crow," said Mockingbird.
"You are not supposed to sing pretty songs."

"When the other birds hear my caw,
they all make fun of it and run away.
I just want someone to play with."

Papa Crow gave in. "It's okay, I suppose."

Mockingbird gave up. "Here, have one."

Very grateful, Little Crow took the seed.
Immediately, he flew to the big old maple tree.

"Oh, no!" chimed all the birds. "It's Little Crow!"

Then, Little Crow took a deep breath,
opened his beak, and sang the same songs
Mockingbird had the night before.

"Per-CHIC-o-ree!"
chirped the finches. *"Cheers to Little Crow."*

"Fee-beee,"
said Phoebe Flycatcher. *"You're good!"*

"What-CHEER!"
said Cardinal. *"Sing with us."*

And Little Crow did.
He closed his eyes and sang with the birds like never before.

As the birds sang, a large shadow flew overhead.

"It's Hawk!" yelled Blue Jay.
"Fly! Too-loo!" he called,
and all the birds soared away.

All except Little Crow.
He didn't hear the alarm.
He sang and trilled.
When he opened his eyes,
Hawk was flying straight at him.

Little Crow's heart fluttered.
His feathers trembled.
But there was no time to take flight.

Hawk snatched Little Crow in his talons and flew toward his nest.

"Per-CHIC-o-ree! Heeelllllp!"

"Poor Finch," said Papa.

"Fee-beee! Help me!"

"Poor Phoebe Flycatcher!" said Papa Crow.

"What-CHEER!" called Little Crow.

"Cardinal?" said Papa Crow. "I am confused."

"Whip-poor-will! Whip-poor-will!"
yelled a desperate and frightened Little Crow.

Why doesn't Papa bring the other crows and save me?
wondered Little Crow.
He said he could find me anywhere when he heard my...Oh!

Little Crow spit out the seed and, at last, let out a loud
"Caaaw!!!"

"It's Little Crow!" Papa called.

The entire flock of crows took to the air.
When they caught up to the hawk,
they swooped down like a black cloud.

The hawk let loose of Little Crow
as the crows chased him away.

"I love your sweet caw so much," crooned Papa Crow.
"I knew just where to find you."

"Oh, Papa," cried Little Crow, still shaking.

Papa hugged Little Crow, and sang an old crow lullaby.
Little Crow quickly joined in.
To the other birds, they sounded out of tune,
but Little Crow didn't care one little bit.

♫♪ FUN FACTS

The birds in *Song for Papa Crow* are common to North America.

American Crow

The crow is a very smart and loyal bird. The entire murder will come to help an injured crow. A "murder" is the word for a group of crows. The male crow often mates for life, and the father crow takes care of its offspring longer than any other animal besides humans. Its call is "caw," but crows can mimic the sounds of animals and humans.

Bluebird

When you see this pretty bird and hear its beautiful song, you know that spring has come. Among its calls are "chur-lee," "tu-a-wee," and "chit-chit-chit."

Blue Jay

The Blue Jay is related to the crow family and is a very clever bird. The jay uses the acid produced by ants to clean fleas off its feathers by "bathing" in ants' nests and letting ants crawl on its body. It chases predators like hawks and owls, and warns small birds by sounding alarm calls like "too-loo" and "jay-jay."

Flycatcher

There are various kinds of flycatchers in the Northeastern United States, among them the Phoebe, whose call is "fee-bee." Some flycatchers nest in trees' cavities and use snake skin for their nests.

Goldfinch

The finch loses its yellow feathers when its breeding season ends. In spring, the male finch becomes bright yellow again. Finches fly in an up-and-down-circular motion like a roller coaster. One of their calls is "per-chic-o-ree."

Hawk

The hawk is a clever and majestic bird. In Song for Papa Crow, the hawk appears to be the villain; however, in nature this predator is simply part of the food chain. Among its calls are "kee-argh" and "kah."

Hummingbird

The small hummingbird is the only bird that can fly backwards and hover. The buzz of its wings sounds like a helicopter. Hummingbirds use silk from spider webs and soft plant down to build their tiny nest. Its call is "chip."

Mockingbird

The mockingbird is a great singer who can imitate the sounds of other birds and animals. It is one of the few birds that can be heard singing at night. Among its songs are "chack," "chair," and "whip-poor-will."

Owl

The owl has huge eyes to help with its night vision. It cannot move its eyes to look sideways — instead, the owl swivels its head around to look backwards and upside-down. Some owls have one ear bigger than the other to help them detect the direction of sounds. The owl's call is "hoo-hoot."

Red Cardinal

The cardinal sometimes fights its own reflection in windows, thinking that it's an intruder. The female cardinal is one of the few female birds that sing, usually from its nest. The cardinal sings almost all year round. It can raise and lower its crest. Among its calls are "what-cheer" and "pret-ty pret-ty."

Woodpecker

The woodpecker is a climbing bird. It has a sharp beak that helps it dig insects from tree bark. Woodpeckers drum with their beaks on the tree to attract mates. When they nest, they will hammer on different surfaces to make noise.